Welcome to
The Giggle Club

The Giggle Club is a collection of picture books made to put a giggle into early reading. There are funny stories about a contrary mouse, a dancing fox, a turtle with a trumpet, a pig with a ball, a hungry monster, a laughing lobster, an elephant who sneezes away the jungle and lots more! Each of these characters is a member of **The Giggle Club**, but anyone can join: just pick up a **Giggle Club** book, read it and get giggling!

Turn to the checklist on the inside back cover and tick off the Giggle Club books you have read.

TEE HEE!

HA HA!

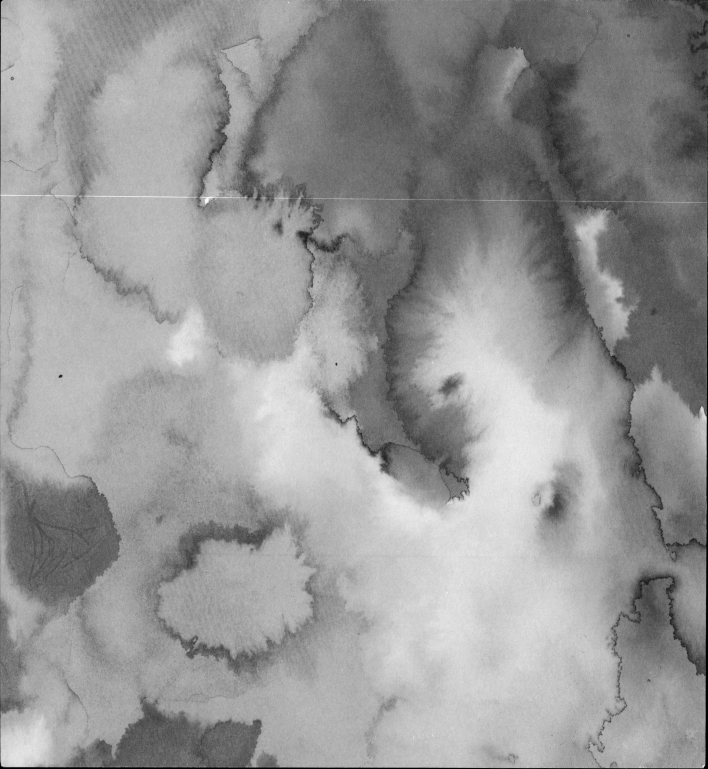

For Deirdre

First published 1995 by Walker Books Ltd
87 Vauxhall Walk, London SE11 5HJ

This edition published 1997

10 9 8 7 6 5

© 1995 Colin West

This book has been typeset in Plantin.

Printed in China

British Library Cataloguing in Publication Data:
a catalogue record for this book is
available from the British Library

ISBN 0-7445-4785-7

www.walkerbooks.co.uk

"ONLY JOKING!" LAUGHED THE LOBSTER

COLIN WEST

WALKER BOOKS
AND SUBSIDIARIES
LONDON • BOSTON • SYDNEY

"Only joking!" laughed the lobster.

"Only joking!" laughed the lobster.

"Only joking!" laughed the lobster.

"Only joking!" laughed the lobster.

"Only joking!" laughed the lobster.